CAUGHT UP

by

SHALONDA REESE

Inquiries concerning rights to production of the play should be addressed to thestoryteller7777@gmail.com.

SPECIAL NOTE

Anyone receiving permission to produce CAUGHT UP is required to give credit to the Author as sole and exclusive Author of the Play on the title page of all programs distributed in connection with performances of the Play and in all instances in which the title of the Play appears for purposes of advertising, publicizing or otherwise exploiting the Play and/or a production thereof. The name of the Author must appear on a separate line, in which no other name appears, immediately beneath the title and in size of type equal to 50% of the size of the largest, most prominent letter used for the title of the play. No person, firm, or entity may receive credit larger or more prominent than that accorded the Author.

CHARACTERS

Mazilya Yarborough (Mazie)--- female, 29, easy-going, entrepreneur
Benjamin Ballard (Benji) --- male, 32, ambitious, accountant
Pastor Lawrence Fuller--- male, 35, very kind, authoritative
Georgette Smith --- female, 30, fun-loving
Jessica Hammond --- female, 26
David Brumms --- male, 28, flirt, charming
Francine McCullough/Customer 1 --- female, 50, elegant
Ms. Isaac --- female, 70, fraud
Larry Smith/Customer 2 --- male, 60
Osvald Emilius --- male, 30+, European accent, charming voice
News Reporter --- female, 25+
TV Preacher --- male, 40 +
Trumpet Man --- male, 30 +
Official 1 --- male or female, 50+
Official 2 --- male or female, 50+
Military Officials --- male, 30+
Wailing woman
Woman with missing son
Man with cane
Man
Woman
Woman 2
Woman 3
Man
Man 2
Man 3
Man 4

It is recommended that the cast double where needed.

NOTE TO THE DIRECTOR:

Most of the scenes are abstract. No set is needed with the exception of Mazie's kitchen and couch and the chairs for the church scene. Sound effects are strongly encouraged. The passage of time is to be assumed accordingly. The director has the creative license to make the scenes as believable as possible without changing the dialogue.

CAUGHT UP

ACT ONE

Scene 1

The stage is dim. Light shines on stage right and stage left. Mazilya enters stage right wearing pajamas and carrying her cell phone. It is late at night and Mazilya is uptight. The phone rings. Benjamin, sleepily, enters stage left with his cell phone.

BENJAMIN: What's wrong, Mazie?

MAZIE: I had the dream again.

BENJAMIN: *(irritated)* What dream?

MAZIE: The same one I've been having. The one about the man standing on the street playing a melody on a trumpet.

BENJAMIN: *(sighing heavily)* Why don't you get one of those dream books?

MAZIE: A book can't tell me what my dreams mean?

BENJAMIN: I don't know what to tell you.

MAZIE: What do you think it means?

BENJAMIN: Maybe the man is waiting for you to talk to him. Next time you have the dream, talk to him, and see what he has to say.

MAZIE: This is not funny, Benjamin.

BENJAMIN: I'm being serious. This happens at night, right?

MAZIE: At dusk.

BENJAMIN: Nobody's on the street but you and this guy. No cars. Nothing. This dude is standing on the street corner holding a trumpet. You stare at him. He stares at you.

Benjamin is silent for a moment.

MAZIE: Benjamin?

BENJAMIN: I'm here. I was just thinking. Are you running from something? Something you're avoiding or don't want to face?

MAZIE: No! I'm not running from anything.

BENJAMIN: Are you sure?

MAZIE: Do you not believe me?

BENJAMIN: If you keep having the same dream, then that means you need to scrutinize your life and your past.

MAZIE: Alright, Benji. I don't know what to think at this point. It's actually a creepy dream. Sorry, I woke you.

BENJAMIN: I'm used to it. Love you.

MAZIE: Love you too.

BENJAMIN: Can't wait to marry you.

MAZIE: One hundred ninety-two days.

LIGHTS DIM

ACT ONE

Scene 2

There are sounds of cars passing by, honking and children playing in the park. It is Georgette's birthday, and her friends are celebrating in the park. Georgette, a pretty, brown-skinned woman with shoulder-length hair and a great smile, wears a yellow dress. Jessica and David, friends of Georgette sit on the bench laughing and talking as Mazie approaches.

GEORGETTE: Hi, Mazie!

MAZIE: Hi, Georgette. Happy birthday (*carrying Georgette's cake*).

GEORGETTE: (*hugging Mazie*) Awwww, thanks Mazie. What kind of cake is it?

MAZIE: The kind you asked for. Lemon Butter.

GEORGETTE: Oooooooohh yeeaaaahhhh!

Everyone laughs.

GEORGETTE: Where are my manners? Mazie, this is Jessica Stewart. Jessica, this is my friend, Mazilya Yarborough, but we just call her Mazie.

JESSICA: Nice to mee you, Mazie.

MAZIE: Likewise, Jessica.

GEORGETTE: And you know David.

MAZIE: Hi, David.

DAVID: Hi, Mazie. Looking good.

MAZIE: Thanks.

JESSICA: Georgette tells me you have your own baking business.

MAZIE: I'm just getting it off the ground. I bake cakes, cupcakes, cookies and all types of pastries and sell them.

GEORGETTE: How much do I owe you?

MAZIE: It's your birthday, Georgette.

GEORGETTE: Before I cut this cake, you need to sing happy birthday to me.

Everyone sings 'Happy Birthday.'

DAVID: Make a wish.

GEORGETTE: Hmmmmmm. My wish is made. Who wants the first slice?

JESSICA: How is it going for you? Do you get a lot of business?

MAZIE: It's picking up some. I have been baking for years as a hobby. I decided that since I get so many requests for food, I may as well make money.

DAVID: I know this is going to be good. Mazie makes the best cakes.

MAZIE: Awwww, thanks David. Between you and Georgette, I'll never go out of business. (*to Jessica*) Do you bake?

JESSICA: (*laughing*) Oh no, that's not my talent. I'm not much of a kitchen type.

MAZIE: What do you do?

JESSICA: I work as a teaching assistant at Clayton Elementary.

MAZIE: Oh, so that's how you know David and Georgette?

JESSICA: Yeah, I just finished my first year there.

MAZIE: How did it go for you?

JESSICA: (*laughing*) It went.

DAVID: Man, this is good. My birthday can't get here quick enough. I will request a special birthday cake from you, Mazie.

MAZIE: David. I want to be clear. I am engaged. You know that.

DAVID: But you ain't married.

GEORGETTE: Boy, if you don't stop!

JESSICA: Congratulations.

MAZIE: Thank you.

JESSICA: When is the wedding?

MAZIE: Saturday after Christmas.

JESSICA: (*excited*) A Christmas wedding.

GEORGETTE: I'm the maid of honor.

MAZIE: I wanted a Christmas wedding. And since my family and his family will be in town for the holidays, we thought it would be best to have it then.

GEORGETTE: Hey Lawrence. Oops. I guess I should say Pastor Lawrence.

Pastor Lawrence is seen approaching holding an envelope.

PASTOR: (*laughing*) You can call me Lawrence. This is for you. Happy Birthday.

GEORGETTE: I love gifts. I'll open it now.

PASTOR: I'm Lawrence Fuller. And you are?

MAZIE: Mazilya Yarborough, but you can call me Mazie.

PASTOR: Mazilya. What a beautiful name.

MAZIE: Thank you.

PASTOR: (*to Jessica*) Lawrence Fuller.

JESSICA: Jessica Hammond.

GEORGETTE: Thank you, Lawrence.

JESSICA: What did you get?

GEORGETTE: A gift certificate to Christian Life Bookstore.

JESSICA: Oh, nice.

GEORGETTE: Have a seat, Lawrence and get a slice of cake. Lawrence is a pastor now. He is starting his own church.

JESSICA: Oh great. I would definitely like to come.

PASTOR: That's great, Jessica. Our first service is going to be tomorrow night at seven upstairs of the Brodiac Complex in room two.

GEORGETTE: I'll be there.

DAVID: Jessica, you can ride with me if you want to go.

JESSICA: Thanks, David. I appreciate it.

PASTOR: You're invited, Mazilya.

MAZIE: Thank you for the invitation.

PASTOR: I'll take a slice to go. I can't stay. I have some things to do and just wanted to stop by and give you your gift.

GEORGETTE: Mazie baked the cake. She's a baker.

PASTOR: Oh, well now. It looks great. I hope to see you tomorrow night, Mazilya.

Pastor Lawrence exits.
It is two hours later and David and Jessica leave as Mazie helps Georgette clean up.

DAVID: See you guys, later.

JESSICA: Take care.

David and Jessica exit together.

GEORGETTE: Are you going to go?

MAZIE: Don't know.

GEORGETTE: Come on, Mazie. What do you have against church?

MAZIE: I don't have anything against church. I grew up in the church.   You know that.

GEORGETTE: Then, what's the problem?

MAZIE: I'm not sure I one hundred percent believe. I have doubts.

GEORGETTE: What exactly don't you believe?

MAZIE: I'm not sure there is a heaven and hell. I am not sure if I believe that Jesus is going to come back and all that stuff they teach in church. That's all.

GEORGETTE: (*disappointed*) Oh. (*a moment of silence*) Just remember this: if I am wrong about there being a heaven and hell, then I have nothing to lose, but if you're wrong, you have a lot to lose. Thanks again for the cake.

LIGHTS DIM

ACT ONE

Scene 3

Mazie is in her kitchen stage right, and Customer 1 is stage left. Mazie's kitchen is simple with bowls, utensils and boxes cake mix. They speak on their phones.

MAZIE: What type of icing would you like?

CUSTOMER 1: What do you have?

MAZIE: I have buttercream, strawberry, chocolate, chocolate berry, mint, lemon cream, cinnamon spice, and caramel vanilla.

CUSTOMER 1: Chocolate berry sounds delicious.

MAZIE: Chocolate berry it is! It's my best-selling one.

CUSTOMER 1: How much is that?

MAZIE: Twenty-five. For two-layer. Three-layer is an extra ten.

CUSTOMER: Can you do a three-layer please?

MAZIE: Sure. Three-layer, chocolate berry and strawberry-flavored cake, correct?

CUSTOMER 1: That is correct.

MAZIE: Wonderful, Ms. McCullough. I will have this ready for you on Tuesday. You can stop by and pick it up.

CUSTOMER 1: Is this your address on your card?

MAZIE: Yes, that's my address on the card.

There is a knock at the door.

MAZIE: How about two PM?

CUSTOMER: That's perfect for me.

MAZIE: Great. I'll see you then. Have a good one.

CUSTOMER: See you then.

Customer 1 exits stage left. Mazie opens the door. Benjamin stands at the door holding a bag.

BENJAMIN: I bought us lunch.

MAZIE: Well, hello to you.

BENJAMIN: Hello, my dear. I hope you are hungry.

Benjamin kisses Mazie on her forehead as he enters.

MAZIE: What did you bring?

BENJAMIN: Chicken sandwiches and fruit.

MAZIE: (*skeptical*) Sounds healthy. Did you make it?

BENJAMIN: Yeah, something like that. What colors did you decide on?

MAZIE: I'm thinking evergreen and champagne.

BENJAMIN: Nice. Christmasy! I like it.

MAZIE: That's not the reason I chose the colors. I just think those colors would go well together for a winter wedding.

BENJAMIN: Let's eat.

MAZIE: I'll pass for right now.

BENJAMIN: You think you're too good to eat my sandwich?

MAZIE: I'll eat it later.

Benjamin turns on the television. The TV Preacher appears stage left and positions himself downstage center facing the audience. He wears a suit and tie.

TV PREACHER: And then shall many be offended, and shall betray one another, and shall hate one another. And many false prophets shall rise, and shall deceive many. And because iniquity shall abound, the love of many shall wax cold. But he that shall endure unto the end, the same shall be saved. And this gospel of the kingdom shall be preached in all the world for a witness unto all nations; and then shall the end come. Matthew twenty-fourth chapter, tenth through the fourteenth verses. (*To audience*) Saints, we are living in perilous times. You see the evidence every day that we are living in the last days. Earthquakes in divers places, wars and rumors of wars. Be vigilant and stay ready for you know not the hour that the Lord cometh. We must be ready at all times.

Benjamin cuts off the television. TV Preacher exits stage left.

BENJAMIN: Making me want to get back in church.

MAZIE: Some preacher that Georgette knows invited me tonight to his first service.

BENJAMIN: First service?

Mazie pours juice in a glass.

MAZIE: Yeah, he's starting a church. Lawrence. I believe he said his last name was Fuller.

BENJAMIN: Lawrence Fuller? Mid-height, with brown skin. Light weight?

MAZIE: Yeah, that's him. How do you know him?

BENJAMIN: I don't know him like that. All I know is that he used to date one of my cousins. Tasha. You met Tasha at the family reunion. Tall lady with the hazel eyes.

MAZIE: Yeah, I remembered Tasha. I really liked her.

BENJAMIN: He broke up with her so I heard once he got saved an all saying that they couldn't be unequally yoked.

MAZIE: Hmmmmmm. Here you go (*handing him the glass*).

Benjamin sips the juice.

BENJAMIN: Are you going?

MAZIE: I was thinking about it.

BENJAMIN: I'll go with you. I don't think he'll remember me though. When I met him, it was just in passing.

MAZIE: Do you believe there is a heaven and a hell?

BENJAMIN: Where is this coming from?

MAZIE: It's just a question, Benji.

BENJAMIN: I've never known you to talk religion.

MAZIE: It's not religion.

BENJAMIN: My grandma used to talk about Jesus coming back before she passed. There may be something to it. Too many have talked about it since he walked the earth. Do you believe in heaven and hell and Jesus coming back?

MAZIE: I don't know quite yet if I fully believe in all of this.

BENJAMIN: So you're going tonight to find out?

Mazie sighs deeply.

BENJAMIN: What about your folks? Did they believe in all of that?

MAZIE: I don't know. We never really talked about it. My parents took me to church every Sunday growing up, but it was out of tradition. They didn't get involved in the church like that. After a while, my dad stopped going. My mother would go sometimes. They didn't talk to me in depth about God. Just typical talk like if I get sick, they would tell me to pray, but nothing else really. I don't remember the last time I've been in a church. Oh, yes, I do. Two years ago, my neighbor, Pam, who lived across from me invited me to a Christmas program at her church. I went. It was nice. I haven't been back. I have to admit. I think about heaven and hell from time to time. The rapture. It's haunting.

BENJAMIN: Wow. It's something to think about for sure. You're scared?

MAZIE: Scared of what?

BENJAMIN: Nothing.

LIGHTS DIM

ACT ONE

Scene 4

The Pastor stands centerstage facing the audience. The congregation sit facing the left and right sides of the pastor. There are a chorus of 'AMENS' as Pastor Lawrence speaks.

PASTOR: Jesus' blood washes us clean. If it wasn't for his blood, we would have no chance at eternal life.   For God so loved the world, that he gave his only begotten Son. That whosoever believeth on him, should not perish but have everlasting life. God sent his Son not in the world to condemn the world but that the world through him might be saved. But men loved darkness rather than light because their deeds were evil.

Mazie shuffles in her chair. Benjamin notices it.

BENJAMIN: (*whispering*) Are you alright?

MAZIE: (*whispering*) Yes.

PASTOR: I had a classmate once back when we were in high school. They called him 'Preacher Man'. Some of the students would scoff and mock him because he didn't participate in the typical teenage stuff, like smoking, trying to get with as many girls as possible. He was all about God. One day, some of the fellas wanted to test him. They brought a fake gun to school and pulled him in the locker room after lunch. They put the fake gun to his head. He thought it was real. They told him to deny Jesus, or they would pull the trigger. He was so scared that he peed his pants right there on the spot. After he peed his pants, a calm came over him. He looked the guy in the eye and said these exact words: "Fear not them which are able to kill the body but not the soul, but rather fear him which is able to destroy both body and soul in hell." The guy with the gun trembled a bit when he said that. After a moment, he put the gun down and apologized for what he did. 'Preacher Man' went to the office immediately afterwards and told the principal what happened. The guys got expelled from school. How do I know the details of how this happened? I was there. I was one of the guys watching. That moment changed me. 'Preacher Man' had no fear at all because of the faith he had in Jesus. That's what I wanted. I wanted what 'Preacher Man' had.

GEORGETTE: Praise the Lord.

PASTOR: Is there anyone here who wants to give Christ a chance? If so, come to the altar. We know not the day nor the hour for his return. You may never get another chance.

BENJAMIN: (*whispering*) I'm going to the altar.

PASTOR: Don't wait until it's too late. There is nothing in this world worth your soul. Nothing. God loved you so much that he sent his only Son to shed his blood so that YOU can have eternal life. That's love. That's love.

Benjamin goes to the altar. Jessica follows behind him. Mazie chokes back a cry. The Pastor looks over at Mazie who refuses to make eye contact with him.

PASTOR: The day you hear his voice, harden not your heart. Anyone else? (*Pause*) For those of you who have come to the altar, this is the most important decision of your life. To follow Christ. You must believe with all your heart. Repeat after me. Lord, I'm a sinner, and I'm sorry for my sins.

JESSICA/BENJAMIN: Lord, I'm a sinner, and I'm sorry for my sins.

PASTOR: Please forgive me for all my sins. I believe in my heart that Jesus is the Son of God.

JESSICA/BENJAMIN: Please forgive me for all my sin sins. I believe in my heart that Jesus is the Son of God.

PASTOR: I believe that he died and was resurrected. I ask, Jesus, that you live in me and be the head of my life.

JESSICA/BENJAMIN: I believe that he died and was resurrected. I ask, Jesus, that you live in me and be the head of my life.

PASTOR: Thank you Lord. In Jesus name we pray, Amen. Go in peace. In the name of our Lord Jesus Christ, you are new creatures in Christ. Welcome to the family of Christ.

Georgette and a few others stand up and applaud.

LIGHTS DIM

ACT TWO

Scene 1

It is late morning, two days later, and Mazie is in her kitchen putting the last finishing touches on a cake. The phone rings as Benjamin enters stage left.

MAZIE: Hello.

BENJAMIN: Hey love.

MAZIE: I didn't hear from you yesterday. That's a first. You never go a day without calling.

BENJAMIN: I'm sorry, babe. I texted you last night though when I got in. I was meeting with Pastor Lawrence all evening.

MAZIE: (*tentatively*) About what?

BENJAMIN: My new life. I even feel different. I'm trying to learn as much as I can. I spent the whole morning reading the bible. I have a lot of learning and growing to do. I'm on my break now at work. What are you up to today? Baking?

MAZIE: I'm finishing up this cake for a customer who is coming to pick it up at two.

BENJAMIN: Must be nice being able to work from home.

MAZIE: It has its pros and cons. Are you coming over tonight?

BENJAMIN: I was planning on attending prayer service tonight.

MAZIE: Prayer service?

BENJAMIN: Yeah. Pastor Lawrence designated Tuesday nights at seven for prayer. I can come over afterwards.

MAZIE: Okay. I guess.

BENJAMIN: I'll text you when I'm on my way over.

LATER THAT DAY

There is a knock at the door as Mazie cleans her kitchen. Francine who is Customer 1 appears. She is around 50 and is very stylish.

FRANCINE: Hello, you must be Mazilya.

MAZIE: I am. Ms. McCullough, right?

FRANCINE: Call me Francine.

MAZIE: Francine, come in.

FRANCINE: Is my cake ready?

MAZIE: It most certainly is. Just come take a look at it to make sure it's pleasing to your sight.

FRANCINE: I hope it tastes as good as it looks. That would be twenty-five, right (*handing her cash*)?

MAZIE: That is correct. Let me get you a receipt.

Mazie grabs her receipt book and pen from the corner counter and writes a receipt. Francine tries to pick up her cake.

MAZIE: Let me help you with that.

FRANCINE: Thank you.

MAZIE: Who's the cake for?

FRANCINE: Me!

They both laugh.

FRANCINE: My co-workers raved so much about your cake. I had to get one. I know my husband is going to help himself to this. I'm going to let him know that I didn't get it for him. Because if I don't tell him that, he'll think it's for him and eat all of it. He may want to come get his own.

MAZIE: Not a problem. Just let me know if he does. I can use all the business I can get.

FRANCINE: I'll pass the word about your cake. Do you have any business cards?

MAZIE: Oh, sure. I should have thought of that myself. Just a minute.

Mazie locates her business cards that are in a basket on the kitchen counter.

FRANCINE: Just stick them down in the side of my purse.

Mazie sticks a few of the cards in her purse.

MAZIE: I most certainly thank you for your business. Enjoy your cake.

FRANCINE: I will. Thanks darling.

MAZIE: Leave a review for me on Facebook, please.

FRANCINE: I will. God bless.

Francine exits. The phone rings. Customer 2 enters stage left on his phone.

MAZIE: Hello.

CUSTOMER 2: Is this Mazie's Bakery?

MAZIE: Yes. This is Mazie's Bakery.

CUSTOMER 2: You just answered the phone like it wasn't. Like you at home watching T.V.

MAZIE: Oh, I'm sorry about that. I do work from home though.

CUSTOMER 2: Alright. I'm calling to see if you bake lemon and pecan pies. By the way, my name is Larry Smith.

MAZIE: Not yet, Mr. Smith. Next year, I will add them.

CUSTOMER 2: Well,......I ain't trying to hurt my wife's feelings or nothing like that, but she ain't never been that good of a cook. Last time, I had family over, she baked one of her infamous pecan pies, and my cousin chipped his tooth biting into it. I had to talk him out of suing us. He was threatening to take the little bit of retirement savings I had. I ain't trying to go down that route again.

MAZIE: How many people are you expecting?

CUSTOMER 2: Twenty-four this time. It's our family reunion.

MAZIE: What about pastries? Many customers order pastries for parties and large gatherings.

CUSTOMER: Okay.

MAZIE: I also bake cookies.

CUSTOMER 2: What kind of cookies?

MAZIE: Strawberry chocolate chip.

CUSTOMER 2: I bet they taste good.

MAZIE: Yes, they do. Also peanut butter caramel chocolate, and blueberry lemon cream.

CUSTOMER 2: (*excited*) They sound delicious. Those are your only flavors?

MAZIE: As of now, those are the only choices for cookies.

CUSTOMER 2: I know some of my family like cookies. I don't know about the rest.

MAZIE: A tart then? I only do raspberry peach shortbread tarts. They are shaped like little squares. About four inches by four inches.

CUSTOMER 2: How about this: Thirty-six strawberry chocolate chip cookies and twenty-four tarts.

MAZIE: That sounds like a plan.

CUSTOMER 2: When can I pick them up?

MAZIE: Come Thursday. I require forty-eight hours from the time the order is placed. The earliest they will be ready is three PM.

CUSTOMER 2: How about Wednesday? My family gets here on Thursday.

MAZIE: If you need it within twenty-four hours, then I double the fee.

CUSTOMER 2: Never mind.

MAZIE: (*laughing*) I assume you have my card.

CUSTOMER 2: No, I got your flyer in the mail.

MAZIE: Oh great. My address is on there. That will be fifty-five dollars. Cash only, Mr. Smith.

CUSTOMER 2: Okay, dear.

MAZIE: I can have them early Thursday morning.

CUSTOMER 2: That will work.

MAZIE: Nine A.M.?

CUSTOMER: I can do that. My family comes in around eleven.

MAZIE: Thank you, and have a good night.

CUSTOMER 2: Good night.

LIGHTS DIM

Scene 2

It is night, and Mazie is asleep on the couch in the den. There is a knock on the door. Mazie jumps up slightly startled and opens the door.

MAZIE: Hey.

BENJAMIN: You were sleeping?

MAZIE: Yes, I fell asleep waiting for you. I don't even know what time it is.

BENJAMIN: It's almost eleven.

MAZIE: You're just making it over here. Was the prayer service that long?

BENJAMIN: Actually, it was only about an hour. I was talking to the pastor afterwards.

MAZIE: Again?

BENJAMIN: Yeah, what do you have to eat?

MAZIE: (*pointing to the plate of food wrapped up on the counter*) You can have the rest.

Mazie positions herself back on the couch. Benjamin takes a moment to devour the food.

MAZIE: (*sarcastically*) Since when do you eat like a gentleman?

BENJAMIN: (*chuckles*) I was just thinking.

MAZIE: About what?

BENJAMIN: Us.

MAZIE: (*cautiously*) What about us?

BENJAMIN: We're unequally yoked now.

MAZIE: Oh, I see. So that's why you've been meeting with Pastor Lawrence, right? Talking about us being unequally yoked.

BENJAMIN: I didn't say that's what we were talking about. I just said we are unequally yoked, but, yes, we did touch on the subject because I told him we were getting married. I want to marry you. But as a follower of Christ, the woman I marry has to be a follower of Christ also.

MAZIE: So what are you saying?

BENJAMIN: You can accept Christ right now in your life.

MAZIE: So you're forcing me to get saved just to be with you.

BENJAMIN: I'm not forcing you. I simply suggested that you do so. The bible speaks about being unequally yoked. We are not married yet and since we are not yet married, we are unequally yoked now.

MAZIE: Are you saying that if I don't accept Christ, you won't marry me?

Benjamin is silent.

MAZIE: Okay. That's my answer.

BENJAMIN: That's not what I'm saying. I..I...Mazie?

MAZIE: Now that you're saved you think that you have the right to just do me like this as if you are all of a sudden better than me?

BENJAMIN: Hold up. You're going out in left field? I love you, Mazie, but we have to be equally yoked.

MAZIE: What if I don't want to?

BENJAMIN: (*shocked*) Then....we can't.....get married.

There is a long silence.

MAZIE: Here take it.

Mazie takes off the engagement ring.

BENJAMIN: Keep the ring. I don't want it back. Keep it.

There is an uncomfortable silence.

MAZIE; You have to get up early for work, don't you? It's late.

BENJAMIN: Yeah, I do. Are you busy all day tomorrow?

MAZIE: Pretty much.   Everything just happened so quickly. It's amazing how life is. Get a curveball when you least expect it.

BENJAMIN: Yeah, you're right. I'll call you tomorrow.

MAZIE: Good night.

Benjamin exits.

LIGHTS DIM

ACT TWO

Scene 3

Three months later

*Benjamin enters stage left. He kneels on the floor with hands
in prayer position.*

BENJAMIN: Lord, I'm asking you to lead me. I love Mazie. I don't
know if I did the right thing. Help me, please. Amen.

*Benjamin exits. Mazie is on the phone with Ms. Isaac. She sits on the
couch with the bible on her lap.*

MAZIE: Ms. Isaac. I finished early with your cake. I'll be home all
day, so you can pick it up earlier than three if you so desire. If not,
I'll see you at three. Have a good day.

*Mazie hangs up her phone. She flips through the pages and starts to
read.*

MAZIE: *I am become a fool in glorying; ye have compelled me: for I
ought to have been commended of you: for in nothing am I behind
the very chiefest apostles, though I be nothing…..(sighing)* I don't
even understand this. *The Lord knoweth how to deliver the godly
out of temptations, and to reserve the unjust unto the day of
judgment to be punished….*judgment to be punished.

There is a knock on the door.

MS. ISAAC: (*off stage*) It's Ms. Isaac, baby. Open up the door.

Mazie opens the door laughing. Ms. Isaac enters. She is 70, outspoken, and nosey.

MAZIE: You know how to announce yourself, Ms. Isaac.

MS. ISAAC: I've been on my feet all morning. Is business booming?

MAZIE: I've been picking up orders, but my business is mostly word of mouth.

MS. ISAAC: You need to increase your price too. How are you living off twenty-five dollars a cake?

MAZIE: I'm making it. I don't want to put the prices so high and lose business.

MS. ISAAC: Alright, but it should be forty-five per cake.

MAZIE: That much more?

MS. ISAAC: I feel like I'm robbing you by giving you only twenty-five.

MAZIE: This is your seventh cake, Ms. Isaac. You're one of my favorite customers. You help keep me busy.

MS. ISAAC: These cakes aren't for me.

MAZIE: They aren't? Who are they for?

MS. ISAAC: I work with the elderly. That's what I do in my spare time since I retired last year. On their birthdays, I order a cake from you.

MAZIE: Ms. Isaac, that's wonderful. I'm sure they love that.

MS. ISAAC: I suppose they do. How is that fiancé of yours? I hope I'm getting an invite to the wedding.

MAZIE: (*hesitant*) We called it off.

MS. ISAAC: Oh, no. Well, the nosey part of me wants to ask why.

Mazie is silent.

MS. ISAAC: I understand if you don't want to share. I probably wouldn't either. I guess I'll grab my cake and get going.

MAZIE: Ms. Isaac?

MS. ISAAC: Yes?

MAZIE: Are you a Christian?

MS. ISAAC: Why of course! I've been saved for over forty years. Never looked back. Why do you ask?

MAZIE: How does that work out for you?

MS. ISAAC: It's been obviously working for forty years because I'm still saved. (*Pause*) Did the breakup have something to do with one of you becoming a Christian?

MAZIE: He became a Christian.

MS. ISAAC: And you're not?

MAZIE: Well, I believe in God. I know Jesus existed and all of that. And..........

MS. ISAAC: But he's saved and you're not, right? It's as simple as that. Yes or no?

MAZIE: Yes. He's saved, and I'm not.

MS. ISAAC: I'll tell you this. Salvation is a personal thing. Living for Christ is a decision you will have to make for yourself. The bible does say we are not to be unequally yoked. My husband and I were married for forty-four years before he passed last year. When we first got married, we were partying it up, drinking it up, just having a good time. Then, I had an experience that changed my life. I was in a car accident that almost took my life. I was in the hospital for two weeks fighting for my life. For the first time in my life, I thought about my souls and eternal life and became frightened. I prayed to God on that hospital bed that if he lets me live, I'll serve him for the rest of my life. A week later, I was home cooking and doing my usual household duties. I gave my life to Christ and have been faithful to the Lord ever since. At first my husband said nothing about it, but I could tell he was starting to resent me because I now had something that took his spot. Jesus. He was now number two. I prayed diligently for years for his soul salvation. I stopped partying, but he didn't. To be honest, for a while, I thought that he would want to divorce me since we no longer had fun together like that. He stuck around. We had a solid marriage, had kids, you know the usual. It took fifteen years of praying for him to come around and give his life to the Lord. Now, don't you take fifteen years. I'm sure it'll work itself out.

MAZIE: Thank you for sharing, Ms. Isaac.

MS. ISAAC: We are living in the last days, honey.

Mazie hands Ms. Isaac her cake.

MAZIE: Do you need me to help you to your car?

MS. ISAAC: I don't need any help. If I made it this far, I can make it back.

Mazie laughs.

MS. ISAAC: Good-bye, darling.

MAZIE: Good-bye, Ms. Isaac, and thanks for the continued support.

MS. ISAAC: (*off stage*) Put in my order for next week for the same cake. I'll be here to pick it up. A lot of birthdays this month.

MAZIE: I most certainly will. Take it easy.

Ms. Isaac exits.

MS. ISAAC: (*off stage*) Oh, I'm going to take it easy right after I get down to Lindley Hall, get my round of Bingo in with a drink.

MAZIE: A what?

MS. ISAAC: A drink. Oh, child, don't look so startled. Nobody's perfect. Not even us Christians. I work with old people all day, honey. The Lord understands.

A text message notification is heard.

Mazie retrieves her phone from the kitchen counter and checks the message. Benjamin can use a microphone off the stage behind the scenes.

BENJAMIN: (*off stage*) I would like to see you. I love you.

Mazie ponders a moment and dials Georgette's number. The phone rings. Georgette enters stage left with her phone and a cup of coffee.

GEORGETTE: Hello.

MAZIE: Hi Georgette.

GEORGETTE: How's it going?

MAZIE: I am fine. How are you?

GEORGETTE: About to sit down with some coffee and grade some papers.

MAZIE: Do you have Pastor Lawrence's phone number?

GEORGETTE: (*Pause*) Why do you need his number?

MAZIE: Georgette, he is a pastor. I have a few questions to ask. That's all.

GEORGETTE: I didn't mean it like that. It just took me off guard.

MAZIE: Are you two seeing each other?

GEORGETTE: We are friendly with each other. And I know that you and Benjamin broke off your engagement so –

MAZIE: Wait. Wait. Wait a minute. It's nothing like that.

GEORGETTE: Well, I'm just saying.

MAZIE: Nothing. Just send me the number please.

GEORGETTE: I'll text it to you.

MAZIE: Thank you. And congratulations. On your relationship. If that's what it is.

GEORGETTE: Thank you.

Georgette exits. A text message notification is heard. Mazie checks the phone.

MAZIE: Five, five, five, eight, four, two, one.

Mazie dials the number. The phone rings. Pastor Lawrence enters stage left.

PASTOR: Hello.

MAZIE: Pastor Lawrence?

PASTOR: Yes, who's speaking?

MAZIE: It's Mazilya Yarborough. I met you at Georgette's birthday party at the park a few months ago.

PASTOR: I remember you, Mazilya. You came to our first service.

MAZIE: Yes, I did.

PASTOR: You haven't been back.

MAZIE: (*laughs uncomfortably*) No, I haven't made it back.

PASTOR: What can I do for you?

MAZIE: Ummmmmm....I need to speak with you. I have a few questions....things that are bothering me.......that I'm unsure about.

PASTOR: We have service tonight. Mid-week service. You can come tonight ---

MAZIE: I prefer to speak with you privately.

PASTOR: I understand. I am available at six in the morning. I don't know if you want to be up that early.

MAZIE: I'll be there. That actually works great for me.

PASTOR: Just come to the same room where we had worship service.

MAZIE: Thank you. See you then.

LIGHTS DIM

ACT TWO

Scene 4

Sound effects of wind blowing or crickets chirping are heard.

The stage is still dark. It is night and Mazie is in her bedroom which is offstage. Mazie speaks from offstage using a microphone if necessary.

MAZIE: (*off stage*) God, I don't talk to you much. I know. I, at least, tried to read some of the bible. It's confusing, and I don't understand it. I believe you exist and all, but…….

The alarm goes off.

    LIGHTS UP

ACT TWO

Scene 5

Pastor Lawrence is sitting behind a desk reading his bible. Mazie enters stage left carrying a purse. There is a chair opposite his desk. He stands up when he sees her.

PASTOR: Good morning, Mazilya.

MAZIE: Good morning, Pastor Lawrence.

PASTOR: It's good to see you again.

MAZIE: Likewise. It looks different in here in the morning.

PASTOR: It does?

MAZIE: I've only been in here once before. It just has a different feel, is what I'm trying to say. Not a bad thing, though.

PASTOR: Thanks for being on time.

MAZIE: I'm not going to keep you. I know you are busy and all.

PASTOR: You're not taking up my time.

MAZIE: I'm going to assume that you know Benjamin and I called off our engagement.

PASTOR: He mentioned it.

MAZIE: Did you advise him to do it? It just seemed to have happened out of the blue.

PASTOR: He asked for my advice on what to do. I gave him scripture. Whatever decision he made, he made it on his own.

MAZIE: I'm not here to accuse you of anything. I just don't understand it. That's all. I remember your story of why you became a Christian. A lady who bought a cake from me told her story of why she became a Christian. I don't have one of those stories. Nothing mind blowing has happened to me to motivate me to become a Christian.

PASTOR: Did you ask Benjamin on why he became one?

MAZIE: I barely got a chance. He got saved and then two days later, the engagement was off. I didn't even see it coming.

PASTOR: Not every person who comes to Christ does so because of a mind-blowing experience. Some people simply make the choice to serve him because they want to live for God or because God draws them to him, and they accept the call.

MAZIE: There is something else on my mind. I keep having this recurring dream about a man standing on the opposite side of the street as I'm walking down the street. And he's playing a melody on his trumpet. No cars pass by or people. It's just us on the street, and it's always dark. He just stares at me and play, but here's the strange thing. I had the same dream just last night, and he wasn't playing the trumpet. He was just standing there staring at me, and then he looked up at the sky, and the dream ended.

PASTOR: How long have you had this dream?

MAZIE: A few months off and on. Sometimes I will go weeks without having the dream or I will have the dream a couple times in a week. I would say I've had the dream about seven or eight times now. It's disturbing. I know it means something because I keep having it.

PASTOR: Jesus is knocking at your heart. You refuse to open it up to him.

MAZIE: You think that's what the dream means?

PASTOR: That's the only thing you're running from? Unless there is something else you haven't told me.

MAZIE: No.

PASTOR: Why so dejected?

MAZIE: I feel like people are forcing this on me.

PASTOR: Nobody's forcing it. Not even the Lord above. It's a choice. That's all. If you want to marry Benjamin, then you will have to make that choice. If not, then that's a choice too. It's all about decisions.

Mazie is silent.

PASTOR: It's simple to do. I can pray with you right now if you want to ask Christ into your life.

Mazie puts her head down.

PASTOR: All it takes is a confession of sins, repentance, and faith in Jesus. That's it.

Mazie is still silent.

PASTOR: You don't want to wait too long. Tomorrow is not promised to anyone.

MAZIE: Not now. I have to think about it.

Pastor nods his head in disappointment.

MAZIE: I'll think I'll get going. Thanks for your time, Pastor.

PASTOR: Take care, Mazilya.

LIGHTS DIM

ACT TWO

Scene 6

*It is the same morning, and Mazie has not yet made it home
from her meeting with Pastor Lawrence. Benjamin arrives at Mazie's
house and knocks on her door.*

BENJAMIN: Mazie! It's Benjamin.

The phone rings four times.

BENJAMIN: Come on, Mazie. Pick up.

*The text message notification is heard. The stage goes completely
dark. There is one long trumpet sound effect that lasts for about five
seconds. There is silence for five seconds.*

*There are sound effects of people screaming and cars
crashing. Mazie enters and sees a Benjamin's clothes in front
of her door. She picks them up puzzled.*

MAZIE: (*gasps*) Benja---

Mazie digs in her purse and pulls out her phone.

BENJAMIN: (*off stage*) Mazie, I'm sorry for how I handled our
breakup. Through prayer and self-reflection, I realized that I was
wrong to throw away our relationship without even being patient
and praying to God for your salvation as I should have done. Please
forgive me. Can we-

Mazie runs out to the street looking around.

MAZIE: Benjamin! Benjamin!

A woman appears who is frantic and distraught.

WOMAN: Have you seen my son? He's three. He's light-skinned with dimples. The clothes he had on were on the floor. A blue shirt, and white pants. He's out naked—

MAZIE: Naked? His clothes were left?

WOMAN: Yes.

MAZIE: I...my fiancé...these are his clothes.

WOMAN: I just turned my head for a split second, and he was gone.

Mazie runs back to her house. The woman exits.

Mazie clicks on the television as the news reporter appears stage left and positions herself downstage center and addresses the audience.

NEWS REPORTER: Breaking news. Reports of missing people, mostly children are pouring in. In the past fifteen minutes, there have been reports of people vanishing. Reports are coming in from all over the world.

MAZIE: Georgette!

The news reporter exits. Mazie nervously fumbles with her phone. The phone rings three times before the voicemail comes up.

MAZIE: Georgette, it's Mazie. Give me a call when you get this message, please. There are reports of people missing. I'm checking in on you.

Mazie hangs up the phone and paces back and forth trying to breathe normally.

MAZIE: No, it can't be.

Mazie stops pacing and dials the Pastor's number.

PASTOR: (*off stage*) You have reached Lawrence Fuller. Please leave a -----

Mazie hangs up the phone furiously.

LIGHTS DIM

ACT TWO

Scene 7

*An old man with a cane, dazed, walks down the street.
Mazie is on the street looking   for answers.*

MAN (*talking to himself*) The rapture happened. It was the rapture.
That's why all the children are gone.

MAZIE: No, no, no.

Mazie runs off stage.

LIGHTS DIM.

*Lights come up as Mazie barges in stage left. David sits in the
church room crying. A woman is on the floor wailing in emotional
pain in a corner wailing in emotional pain.*

MAZIE: So it's true. It happened.

David does not look up. He continues to cry in misery.

MAZIE: How could it have happened so soon?

*Mazie's knees drop to the floor. She puts her head in her
hands and begins to cry.*

MAZIE: I waited too late. Oh, God. I didn't believe. I didn't believe.
Ooooohhhhhhhhhh.

DAVID: We missed the rapture. It's nobody's fault but ours. We
have to repent. That's the only way.

MAZIE: (*not looking up*) Georgette?

DAVID: Georgette, Pastor Lawrence, Jessica. They're all gone. (*Pause*) I'm sorry, Lord for rejecting you. I believe now Lord in You and Your Son, Jesus. I believe that he rose from the dead. I ask that you come into my life and guide me forever more. In Jesus' name. Amen.

Mazie rocks back and forth moaning.

DAVID: (*getting on his knees beside Mazie*) Come on, Mazie. You have to believe now. You have to surrender.

MAZIE: Jesus.

Mazie moans and continues to rock back and forth.

DAVID: Say, I'm sorry for my sins.

MAZIE: I'm sorry for my sins.

DAVID: Please forgive me for my sins.

MAZIE: Please forgive me for my sins. I am so sorry I didn't believe.

DAVID: Say, please live in me.

MAZIE: Please live in me.

DAVID: I believe you died for my sins.

MAZIE: I believe you died for my sins.

LIGHTS DIM

Later in the afternoon, David and Mazie are still in the church room. The wailing woman is gone.

DAVID: Just so you know that we now have to go back out in the world to face what's to come. Your fiancé?

MAZIE: He's gone too.

DAVID: Oh……sorry to hear….I mean. I didn't mean it that way. I meant…..well, that's good for him, but not for you….never mind.

MAZIE: I know what you mean, David. Does Pastor Lawrence have a bible here? He should.

Mazie searches the desk and finds a bible in a drawer.

MAZIE: I know that all the end time prophecy is in Revelation.

DAVID: Revelation chapter nine starting with verse two.

Mazie hands him the bible. David flips to the book of Revelation.

DAVID: And he opened the bottomless pit; and there arose a smoke out of the pit, as the smoke of a great furnace; and the sun and the air were darkened by reason of the smoke of the pit. And there came out of the smoke locusts upon the earth: and unto them was given power, as the scorpions of the earth have power.

LIGHTS DIM gradually as they both exit off stage.

David continues to read, and it turns into a voiceover as he reads backstage.

DAVID: (*voiceover*) And it was commanded them that they should not hurt the grass of the earth, neither any green thing, neither any tree; but only those men which have not the seal of God in their foreheads. And to them it was given that they should not kill them, but that they should be tormented five months: and their torment was as the torment of a scorpion, when he striketh a man.

Cars pass by and drivers honk their horns. Voices are heard talking about the rapture. The voices should sound faint but be loud enough for the audience to hear. They can be pre-recorded on tape or the actors can voice them from backstage. The voices should not drown out David's voice as both will happen simultaneously in the following scene.

[The director can decide where to place the voices during David's voiceover.]

VOICES: (*off stage*) Was it really the rapture?/ Alien abduction. I knew aliens were real./ Then why are all the children missing?/ Oh, my Betty.

DAVID: (*off stage*) And in those days shall men seek death, and shall not find it; and shall desire to die, and death shall flee from them. And the shapes of the locusts were like unto horses prepared unto battle; and on their heads were as it were crowns like gold, and their faces were as the faces of men. And they had hair as the hair of women, and their teeth were as the teeth of lions. And they had breastplates, as it were breastplates of iron; and the sound of their wings was as the sound of chariots of many horses running to battle. And they had tails like unto scorpions, and there were stings in their tails: and their power was to hurt men five months.

Mazie enters her home. She puts her purse on the counter and begins to prepare a sandwich to eat.

DAVID: (*off stage*) And they had a king over them, which is the angel of the bottomless pit, whose name is Abaddon, but in the Greek tongue hath his name Apollyon. One woe is past; and behold, there come two woes more hereafter. And the sixth angel sounded, and I heard a voice from the four horns of the golden altar which is before God, saying to the sixth angel which had the trumpet, Loose the four angels which are bound in the great river Euphrates. And the four angels were loosed, which were prepared for an hour, and a day, and a month, and a year, for to slay the third part of men.

Mazie takes the bible from her bedroom and sits on the couch with her sandwich.

DAVID: (*off stage*) Revelation chapter thirteen verse eleven.

Mazie flips the bible open to the book Revelation, and they begin to read simultaneously.

DAVID: (*off stage*)/MAZIE: And I beheld another beast coming up out of the earth; and the had two horns like a lamb, and he spake as a dragon. And he exerciseth all the power of the first beast before him, and causeth the earth and them which dwell therein to worship the first beast, whose deadly wound was healed. And he doeth great wonders, so that he maketh fire come down form heaven on earth in the sight of men. And he deceiveth them that dwell on the earth by the means of those miracles which he had power to do in the sight of the beast; saying to them that dwell on the earth, that they should make an image to the beats, which had the wound by a sword, and did live.

Mazie bites off a huge chunk of her sandwich as she reads silently for a few moments.

DAIVD: (*off stage*) And he had power to give life unto the image of the beast, that the image of the beast should both speak, and cause that as many as would not worship the image of the beast should be killed. And he causeth all, both small and great, rich and poor, free and bond, to receive the mark in their foreheads:

DAVID: (*off stage*)/MAZIE: And that no man might buy or sell, save he that had the mark, or the name of the beast, or the number of his name.

Mazie closes the bible suddenly and clicks on the TV.

DAVID: (*off stage*) Here is wisdom. Let him that hath understanding count the number of the beast: for it is the number of man; and his number is six hundred threescore and six.

Osvald Emilius, a handsome man, 40s, dressed sharply in a suit and tie enters stage left. He positions himself downstage center and addresses the audience.

OSVALD EMILIUS: Our goal is to unite the world into one faith. That would bring about peace.

The phone rings.

OSVALD EMILIUS: The whole world will have one monetary system.

David enters stage left.

DAVID: Are you watching the news?

MAZIE: Yes.

OSVALD EMILIUS: No more division, no more differences. As servants to each other, it is our duty to make it so that we are all on one accord. As your leader, I hope you have the faith that I will do my best to unite all faiths, all religions and all people.

DAVID: This is it.

The TV audience applauds. Osvald Emilius exits.

MAZIE: It's happening so quickly.

DAVID: Are you stocked up with food?

MAZIE: I haven't gone grocery shopping this week.

DAVID: Go out and get as many can goods as you can. I imagine that the stores will be packed. Do this every day for the next few days. Get a bunch of can goods and ramen noodles. I keep a big stock of those. I can bring you some.

MAZIE: I would appreciate that. I live over on –

DAVID: I Know where you live.

MAZIE: You do?

DAVID: I was in the car with Georgette when she stopped by to give you your gift when she couldn't make your engagement party. I just stayed in the car.

MAZIE: Oh.

DAVID: I can come over tonight and bring the can goods.

Mazie hesitates.

DAVID: I'm not trying to take your fiance's place or anything like that.

MAZIE: I think I'll call it a night. I need rest.

DAVID: (*disappointed*) I understand. This lady next to me has been crying all day about her six-year old son who vanished when she was putting him in the car.

MAZIE: Did you tell her it was the rapture?

DAVID: I told her. She won't listen to me. She thinks I'm crazy.

MAZIE: What are you going to do about work?

DAVID: All the kids are gone. The schools are shut down.

MAZIE: You knew exactly where to go in the bible for the end time prophecy. How come you did not accept before?

DAVID: I did.

MAZIE: How come you're still here?

DAVID: I was uhh…..lukewarm…as they call it. I had no problems going to church, but I also went to bars sometimes and got drunk with the fellas.

MAZIE: Thanks for being honest.

DAVID: If there is anything you need, you can call me. Stay strong and read the bible every day.

MAZIE: Okay, but that's it? That's the survival plan?

DAVID: The survival plan is to not accept the mark of the beast when it comes. If you do, you're doomed to the lake of fire. If you don't accept, you are killed, but your spirit goes to be with the Lord.

LIGHTS DIM

ACT THREE

Scene 1

Mazie enters her home carrying a bag of groceries. She positions the bag on the counter begins to remove canned goods from the bag. There is a knock on the door. Mazie freezes.

MAZIE: (*timidly*) David?

MS. ISAAC: (*off stage)* It's Ms. Isaac, baby. Open up.

MAZIE: (*opening the door*) Ms. Isaac? What are you doing here?

MS. ISAAC: (*entering*) I came to pick up my cake.

MAZIE: Oh no. I'm sorry, Ms. Isaac. I completely forgot because of what has been going on. You're still here. I thought you would have been gone. You said that you were a Christian.

MS. ISAAC: (*offended*) I am!

MAZIE: You were left behind like the rest of us.

MS. ISAAC: First of all, I was not left behind. That was not the rapture. Did you not hear Osvald Emilius? That was an alien abduction. He's so handsome. If only I was thirty years younger. You know there are other life forms out there. I'm glad those aliens left me here. I'm too old to be going through those type of changes.

MAZIE: Ms. Isaac, I accepted Christ. You have to accept Christ before it's too late, before you get forced to take the mark of the beast.

MS. ISAAC: (*holding up her right hand*) Do you see this here? Nobody forced me to take anything.

MAZIE: (*shocked*) You took the mark.

MS. ISAAC: Every law-abiding citizen has to get this mark. I just went and got mine to get it out of the way. And by the look of it, you haven't gotten yours yet?

Mazie is silent.

MS. ISAAC: Well, you do know that eventually you will have to get it to continue your bakery business. You bake the best cakes. It would be shame for it to go to waste. And since you don't have my cake, I guess that means it's on the house when you do get it (*chuckles knowingly*).

Ms. Isaac exits as Mazie stares after her. Mazie turns on television. The news reporter enters and positions herself downstage center. She has the mark on her forehead.

NEWS REPORTER: Officials from the Unity Federal Coalition will be contacting individuals who have not yet received the mark. Citizens can go down to any government agency to get the mark. This is WNG reporting.

The news reporter exits. Mazie grabs her cell phone and dials David's number. The phone rings. David enters stage left. He has a mark on his forehead.

MAZIE: Hello, David.

DAVID: (*monotone*) Hi Mazie.

MAZIE: I just saw the news about getting the mark. One of my customers, Ms. Isaac got the mark on her right hand. I thought she was saved. I couldn't believe it. She made it seem so normal. I just can't wrap my mind around all of this.

David is silent.

MAZIE: David?

DAVID: Yes?

MAZIE: (*nervous*) Did you take the mark?

DAVID: It's the only way.

MAZIE: (*in disbelief*) What!!!

Mazie hangs up the phone. Two military men approach are seen approaching. They each have the mark on their foreheads. They slowly and chillingly knock on the door. Mazie shakes in fear.

MAZIE: Lord, please don't let me take the mark. I want to spend eternity with you.

LIGHTS DIM

ACT THREE

Scene 2

[The stage should be completely clear.]

There is a short line of people at the Public Community Station. Mazie is in the middle of the line. There are two officials in white lab coats stamping the right hand or the forehead of the people. They each hold a small instrument in their hands.

MAN: (*off stage*) I will not take this mark. No, no you will have to kill me.

The man screams painfully.

OFFICIAL 1: Where do you want it?

WOMAN: Right hand of course.

The official 2 stamps the woman's right hand.

WOMAN: That wasn't so bad.

OFFICIAL 2: Have a nice day ma'am.

The man screams chilling screams again backstage as the woman exits.

OFFICIAL 2: Good day, sir.

MAN 2: There is nothing hard about being a law-abiding citizen.

MAN: (*off stage*) Aaaaaaarrrrrrgggggghhhhhhh! (defeated) I'll take it.

MILITARY MAN: (*off stage*) Wise choice. It won't hurt.

Official 2 stamps Man 2's forehead.

MAN: (*off stage*) I feel brand new. Have a good day, sir.

MILITARY MAN: (*off stage*) Good day.

The man appears with the mark on his forehead and exits. Man 2 follows behind Man as they both exit.

OFFICIAL 1: Right hand or forehead, Miss?

Mazie is silent.

OFFICIAL 2: Miss, we don't have all day.

Mazie takes off running.

MILITARY MAN: (*off stage*) Oh, no you don't.

MAN 3: (*nervous*) I was told that I shouldn't take the mark.

OFFICIAL 1: I can assure you that it's the best thing for you and this world.

MAZIE: (*off stage*) Aaaaaaarrrrghhhhhhh!

OFFICIAL 2: You don't want to end up like her, do you?

MILITARY MAN: (*off stage*) Make this easy for the both of us, ma'am.

MAZIE: (*off stage*) Aaaaaaarrrrrrrghhhhhhhhh!!!

MAN 3: Put it right smack in the middle of my forehead. It's not worth the trouble.

OFFICIAL 1: Glad you realized that.

Official 2 stamps Man 3's forehead.

MAZIE: (*off stage*) Lord, help me to endure.

MILITARY MAN: (*laughs*) The Lord is not going to help you. You belong to us.

MAZIE: (*off stage*) I belong to Jesus.

As Man 3 exits, Man 4 jumps out of line and runs away.

MAN 4: (*knocking man 3 to the ground*) Out of my way.

OFFICIAL 1: Catch him.

The military man appears on stage and follows behind Man 4. They are now both off stage. Mazie runs onstage, and then runs off-stage.

OFFICIAL 2 (*pulling out walkie-talkie*) We have another runner.

[*STAGE GOES COMPLETELY DARK*]

When the lights come up, only Mazie and the man from her dreams are onstage. He holds a trumpet. He is dressed in a black suit and looks to be about 30. He puts trumpet to his mouth. Man 4 and two other women enter the stage running and crying.

MAZIE: (*amazed*) It's you! Am I dreaming?

The trumpet man says nothing.

WOMAN 2: What are we going to do?

MAN 4: We can't hide from them. They're everywhere.

MAZIE: (*runs over to them*) You must give your lives to Christ. That's your only escape.

The military men's footsteps are heard backstage.

WOMAN 3: They see us!

MAZIE: Just ask Jesus into your heart and to save you. Do it now.

MAN 4/WOMAN 2/ WOMAN 3: Save us Lord. Come into my life, Jesus and save me.

The man blows the trumpet for about a second. The military men enter. The man and two women jump up and down in praise and thanksgiving lifting their arms up to the Lord unaware of the military men who enter looking for them. Mazie watches the military men.

MILITARY MAN 1: Where are they?

MILITARY MAN 2: I saw them from the street. Where did they go?

The military men, confused, move around the stage frantically looking for the people. They do not see the people celebrating, Mazie, nor the trumpet man.

MILITARY MAN 1: Go that way, and I'll go this way.

They exit in opposite directions. Mazie celebrates with the people. The trumpet man stands center stage and addresses the audience with a rich powerful voice.

TRUMPET MAN: For this we say unto you by the word of the Lord, that we which are alive and remain unto the coming of the Lord shall not prevent them which are asleep. For the Lord himself shall descend from heaven with a shout, with the voice of the archangel, and with the trump of God: and the dead in Christ shall rise first: Then we which are alive and remain shall be caught up together with them in the clouds, to meet the Lord in the air: and so shall we ever be with the Lord. First Thessalonians fourth chapter fifteenth through the seventeenth verses.

THE END.